The One Hundredth Day of School!

by ABBY KLEIN

illustrated by
JOHN MCKINLEY

THE BLUE SKY PRESS
An Imprint of Scholastic Inc. • New York

To my colleagues at Franklin Elementary School—
I love you all.
A. K.

THE BLUE SKY PRESS

Text copyright © 2008 by Abby Klein
Illustrations copyright © 2008 by John McKinley
All rights reserved.

Special thanks to Robert Martin Staenberg.

Library of Congress catalog card number 2007030172.
ISBN-10: 0-439-89593-6 / ISBN-13: 978-0-439-89593-4
14 13   12
Printed in the United States of America   40
First printing, January 2008

CHAPTERS

1. Help! 9

2. Twins 18

3. What to Bring? 28

4. One Hundred, One Hundred,
One Hundred 40

5. Suzie to the Rescue? 48

6. Cookie Craziness 57

7. Disaster! 66

8. The Hundredth Day 76

Freddy's Fun Pages 91

I have a problem.

A really, really, big problem.

My teacher told us to bring in

one hundred of something for

the one hundredth day of school,

but I can't think of anything

fun to bring.

Let me tell you about it.

CHAPTER 1

Help!

"Help! Help!" I yelled as I ran into the kitchen in my underwear.

"Freddy, what's the problem?" asked my mom.

"Uh, do you plan on going to school in your shark underwear, Ding-Dong? I think you forgot something . . . like your pants," my sister Suzie said, laughing.

"Ha-ha, very funny. I didn't forget my pants. I have them right here," I said, holding them up.

"Well, could you put them on? I'm trying to eat breakfast here, and I'm losing my appetite seeing you in your tightie whities with sharks all over them."

"That's the problem. I can't put them on."

"Oh, does the little baby waby need help getting dressed?" Suzie cooed.

"No, I don't need help," I said, sticking my tongue out at her.

"Then why don't you put your pants on, sweetheart?" said my mom.

"Because the button fell off, so they won't stay up."

"Then go get another pair, honey."

"I can't."

"Why not?"

"Because I have to wear *these* pants today."

"You're crazy," Suzie mumbled under her breath.

"I heard that," I said, "and I'm not crazy."

"But, Freddy, I don't understand," said my

mom. "Why can't you just go put on another pair of pants?"

"Because today is Twin Day at school."

"So . . . ?"

"So that means you are supposed to come dressed the same as one of your friends."

"Who are you going to dress the same as?" asked Suzie. "Frankenstein?"

"Oh that's so funny I forgot to laugh. No. For your information, I am going to be twins with Robbie."

"Did the two of you decide which dresses you are going to wear?"

"You think you're so funny, don't you?"

"Yeah, I do." Suzie chuckled.

"Robbie and I decided that we would each wear an orange shark shirt, khaki pants, and our black sneakers."

"How original," Suzie said.

"Can't you wear your other pair of khakis?" asked my mom.

"No, I already tried those this morning, and they're too small."

"Well then why don't you call Robbie and ask him to put on a different pair of pants?"

"I can't. He's already left. His mom had to drop him off early."

"Maybe we can pin them."

"That's a great idea, Mom. Just tell me where the pins are, and I'll get one."

"I'm not sure where I put them, sweetie. Let me think."

"Well, think fast, Mom. We don't have all morning," I said, jumping around in my underwear.

"Calm down, Freddy. Give me a minute to think. Why don't you sit and eat your cereal while I look around."

"You want him to eat while he's naked?" said Suzie. "Gross."

"Oh Suzie, he's got his underwear on, for goodness sake. Leave him alone."

I sat down to eat my cereal while my mom searched for a safety pin. I could hear her opening and closing different cabinets and muttering to herself, "Not here. No . . . not here, either."

I had given up hope when my mom came running back into the kitchen. "I found some-

thing better than a pin!" she said happily. My mom held up a little, brown button. "It's one of Grammy Rose's old buttons. I think this will be perfect for your pants, Freddy. It looks like it's just the right size for the buttonhole."

"Really?" I said, feeling hopeful.

"Let's see. Hand me your pants."

I handed my pants to my mom. She tried the button in the hole. "We've got a winner!" she said. "It'll just take me a minute to sew it on."

"Oh yeah, oh yeah, oh yeah," I sang as I did a little dance around the kitchen table.

"Okay, dancing queen, you can sit down now," said Suzie. "I think I'm going to throw up."

I stuck my tongue out at her.

She swatted her hand in my direction. "Get out of here, weirdo."

"All right. Enough, you two," said my mom. "Here, Freddy, I think I'm finished. You can try these on."

I took the pants and slipped them on. I held my breath as I tried the button. It slipped easily into the buttonhole, and my pants stayed up! "It works! It works! Thanks, Mom, you're a genius," I said, giving her a great big hug.

I rubbed my lucky shark tooth, and I pumped my fist in the air. "Now Robbie and I can be twins after all."

CHAPTER 2

Twins

The whole pants crisis almost made me late to school. I got to my classroom just as the final bell was ringing. I hung up my backpack and went to sit down on the rug next to my best friend, Robbie.

"You had me worried, Freddy," said Robbie. "I thought maybe you weren't coming today."

"Yeah, sorry. I had a little crisis this morning."

"Crisis? What kind of crisis? Are you okay?" Robbie asked with a worried look on his face.

"The button on these pants fell off, and my mom had to sew on a new one."

"That was your crisis?"

"Yeah."

"Uh, Freddy, I've got news for you. That's not a crisis."

"It is if it's the only pair of khaki pants you have."

"Why didn't you just put on another pair of pants?"

"Duh . . . because it's Twin Day. We wouldn't look like twins if I were wearing jeans, and you were wearing khaki pants."

"Oh yeah," Robbie said, laughing. "But I'm sure we're the only ones who have matching shark shirts." Then Robbie turned to our friend, Jessie. "So, Jessie, how do Freddy and I look?"

"You guys look great! Just like twins. Those shark shirts are awesome. And you even have the same shoes."

Max, the biggest bully in the whole first grade, butted in. "I think the two of you look stupid."

"Oh, you're just jealous," said Jessie.

"No I'm not!" shouted Max.

"You're jealous because no one would dress up like you for Twin Day."

"Yes they would," said Max. "I didn't want to."

"Sure," said Jessie.

Max scowled at her.

"Maybe if you were a little nicer to people, Max, then they'd want to be your twin."

Max made a fist and shook it in front of Jessie's face. "How would you like a punch in the nose?"

Jessie is so brave, she didn't even flinch.

Just then our teacher, Mrs. Wushy, saw Max out of the corner of her eye.

"Max Sellars! What do you think you're doing?"

Max dropped his fist and looked up at Mrs. Wushy. "Nothing," he said.

"Well, it sure looked like something to me," Mrs. Wushy said. "You need to go sit in a chair right now."

Max slowly got up off the rug and went to go sit in a chair.

"Are you okay, Jessie?" Mrs. Wushy asked.

"Yes, I'm fine," Jessie said, smiling.

When it came to Max, Jessie was always fine. That's because she was the only one in the class who wasn't afraid of him.

Mrs. Wushy walked back to the front of the room. "Good morning, boys and girls. I have to tell you about something special that is going to happen at school this week."

"Are we going to have pony rides at recess?" Chloe asked.

"Pony rides at recess? Where does she come up with this stuff?" I whispered to Robbie.

Robbie shook his head and made the cuckoo sign with his finger.

Mrs. Wushy must have been thinking the same thing because she stared at Chloe for a minute with a strange look on her face, and then she said, "Uh, no, we are not going to have pony rides at recess."

"That's too bad," said Chloe. "I just love ponies. I keep asking my mommy to buy me a little brown one."

"Is there anything she doesn't ask her parents to buy?" Jessie whispered to me.

"I doubt it."

"That girl is so spoiled."

"I know," I said, nodding my head.

"If we had ponies, they'd poop all over the playground," Max blurted out.

"Max, that is not appropriate," said Mrs. Wushy. "OK, everyone, enough talk about ponies. We are not having any ponies at school! Now, as I was saying, something special is happening at school this week. Does anyone know what it is?"

We all stared at Mrs. Wushy with blank looks on our faces.

"I'll give you a hint. Today is the ninety-eighth

day of school, so that means on Wednesday it will be the . . ."

"Hundredth day of school!" we all yelled.

"That's right! Wednesday is the hundredth day of school, and we are going to have a little celebration."

"Hooray, hooray!" we all shouted.

"You mean like a party?" Chloe asked.

"Well, sort of," said Mrs. Wushy.

"Oooo, I love parties!" Chloe squealed.

"Is there anything she doesn't love?" Jessie whispered.

"Yeah, Max Sellars." We both giggled.

"Are we going to have cupcakes, and treats, and decorate the whole room?" Chloe continued.

"It's not exactly that kind of party," said Mrs. Wushy. "That sounds more like a birthday party. At our hundredth-day party we are going to do a lot of activities with the number one hundred."

"Oh," Chloe said, sounding disappointed.

"It's going to be lots of fun. On that day, I would like each of you to bring in one hundred of something."

Robbie raised his hand.

"Yes, Robbie?" said Mrs. Wushy.

"Can we bring in one hundred of anything we want?"

"Yes, as long as you can carry it into the room," Mrs. Wushy said, smiling.

"Boy, that sure is a lot of something," I said. "I'm not sure I have one hundred of anything."

"Sure you do, Freddy. I think you'll be surprised. Remember, one hundred is only ten groups of ten."

"That's true."

"Before you bring in your items, please count them to make sure you have exactly one hundred—no more and no less. Be creative and use your imagination," Mrs. Wushy said.

That's easy for her to say, I thought to myself.

She didn't have to bring in one hundred things. How was I going to find one hundred of something creative in two days? I hit my forehead with the palm of my hand. "Think, think, think."

CHAPTER 3

What to Bring?

"What's wrong, Freddy?" my mom asked that night at dinner. "You haven't touched your food, and I made your favorite—tuna noodle casserole."

"Oh, I bet I know why he's pouting," said Suzie. "Robbie probably forgot it was Twin Day, so Freddy didn't have a twin."

"Wrong! Robbie remembered. In fact, we were the best twins in the class. Everybody said so."

"So then why are you moping?" asked my

dad. "I heard Mom saved the day when the button on your pants came off this morning. I'd think you'd be happy about that."

"I am . . . I mean I was . . . I mean . . ."

"Spit it out, Shark Breath," said Suzie. "What *do* you mean?"

"Suzie," said my dad, "leave Freddy alone."

"What is it, Freddy?" asked my mom. "Why are you upset?"

"Hundredth day!" I blurted out.

"Hundredth day? What does that mean?" asked my dad.

"He's talking about the hundredth day of school," said Suzie.

"When is that?" my mom asked.

"It's on Wednesday," said Suzie.

"Isn't that supposed to be a fun day?"

"Yeah, it's really fun. You get to do a lot of cool activities with the number one hundred. I remember from when I was in first grade."

"So, Freddy, I don't understand. I would think

you'd be excited about this," said my mom. "What's the problem?"

"The problem is that Mrs. Wushy told us to bring in one hundred of something special, and I don't have one hundred of anything cool!" I cried, bending over and covering my head with my hands.

"Freddy, Freddy," said my mom. "Sit up right this minute. We are eating dinner. I don't want you to put your head in your plate. And remember what I said about no elbows on the table."

My mom was such a neat freak.

"Where are your manners?" She gently pulled my head up off the table.

Suzie started laughing uncontrollably and pointed at me. "Ha, ha, ha! That's hilarious . . . ha, ha, ha!"

"What's so funny?"

"You've got . . . you've got . . ."

"I've got what?" I yelled at her.

"You've got a noodle from the tuna noodle casserole hanging from your hair."

"What?" said my mom. She grabbed my chin in her hand and turned me toward her. "Oh my goodness, Freddy. Look what you did! What a mess! Let me find something to clean it," she said, getting up from the table. "And you can stop laughing now, Suzie."

"But it's so funny!"

I pulled the noodle out of my hair and stuck it in my mouth.

My mom came back with a paper towel and a sponge. "Turn and look at me Freddy, so I can get it out of your hair."

"I already did."

"You did? Where is it?"

"I ate it."

"You what?"

"I ate it."

"Ewwww, that's gross," said Suzie.

"You ate it? Freddy, you don't eat things out of your hair!"

My dad snickered.

"Daniel, you're not helping me here," said my mom. "I'm trying to teach Freddy some manners."

"You're right," said my dad. "I'm sorry. Freddy, please do not put your head in your plate while we are eating. And if you do get something in your hair by accident, then you need to go to the sink and wash it out, not eat it! Now, what do you have to say?"

"Sorry, Mom. Sorry, Dad."

"Let me get you a fresh plate," said my mom, taking my dirty plate to the sink. "Tuna noodle casserole tastes a lot better without hair in it."

She brought me a fresh plate of food and set it down in front of me. "Now, Freddy, you start eating, and we'll all help you think of something you can bring for the hundredth day."

"Suzie," my dad asked, "what did you bring when you were in Mrs. Wushy's class?"

"I brought in a necklace I had made with one hundred beads."

"Oh, yes, now I remember," said my mom. "That's a good idea, Freddy. Do you want to do that?'

"No, that's too girly."

"How about your baseball cards?" asked my dad. "You probably have one hundred of those."

"Nah, Max already said he was going to bring in baseball cards. I don't want to copy him. He might get mad."

"Well, you certainly don't want to make *him* mad."

"No way," I said, shaking my head.

"Why don't you bring in one hundred paper clips?" my mom suggested. "I think I have a package of one hundred in my desk drawer. Do you want me to go look?"

"Nah. Paper clips are too boring."

"We could hook them together and make a long chain."

"Thanks, Mom, but I don't want to do that. Mrs. Wushy said to be creative and use our imaginations. Paper clips aren't very original."

"You could bring in one hundred animal crackers," said Suzie.

"Good idea, but they might break before I got them to school." I hit the table with my fist. "Do you see what I mean? I can't think of anything good to bring."

"Freddy, do not bang on the table. You already made one mess tonight. We don't need another one," said my mom.

"Calm down, Freddy. You'll think of something," my dad said.

"But I only have two days, and I want to think of something really good."

My dad chuckled.

"Why are you laughing, Dad? It's not funny."

"I just had a great idea."

"You did? What is it? Tell me! Tell me!"

"You know that real shark jaw Mom and I got you last Christmas?"

"Yeah?"

"Why don't you bring that?"

"Bring that? What are you talking about, Dad? I only have *one* shark's jaw, not one hundred!"

"I know, but I bet that jaw has one hundred teeth in it."

"What a great idea, Dad! I'm going upstairs to get it right now!" I jumped up from my chair and ran out of the kitchen. In a flash, I was back with the shark's jaw in my hands. I set it down on the table. "Do you want to help me count?"

"Sure, we'll all help," said my mom.

We all started counting together. "One, two, three . . ." We counted slowly because we didn't want to miss a tooth. It took a while, but finally we were close to the end, "Ninety-six, ninety-seven, ninety-eight."

"Ninety-eight! Oh no! That can't be right. Let me count again!"

I counted all over again and still came out with ninety-eight.

I shoved my chair back from the table and stood up. "I'll never have one hundred of anything good! Never!" I shouted and ran out of the room.

CHAPTER 4

One Hundred, One Hundred, One Hundred

The next day on the bus everyone was talking about what they were going to bring for the big hundredth-day celebration.

"I'm going to bring one hundred baseball cards," said Max.

"We know," said Chloe. "You already told us yesterday."

"No I didn't!" Max yelled in her face.

Chloe pinched her nose closed. "P.U. Stinkyhead. Your breath stinks. You need to brush your teeth."

"What did you say to me?" Max said, grabbing Chloe's arm.

"Oww, you're hurting me. Let go!"

"Not until you tell me what you said."

Chloe squirmed in her seat. "Let me go, you big bully."

Max just laughed.

"Let me go, or I'll tell Mrs. Wushy when we get to school, and she'll send you to the principal's office."

Chloe must have said the magic words because Max let go of her arm.

"I guess he and Mr. Pendergast have been seeing a lot of each other lately," I whispered to Robbie.

"Yeah, he could probably find his way to the office with his eyes closed, he's been there so many times."

When the bus stopped to pick up some other kids, Chloe moved away from Max and went to sit next to Jessie. "So Jessie, what are you bringing tomorrow?"

"It's a surprise. It's a special collection that belongs to my *abuela*, my grandmother. She got them in Guatemala. I counted them last night. She actually has over one hundred, but I'll just

bring one hundred. I know Mrs. Wushy said no more and no less."

"Lucky," I mumbled to myself.

"I'm bringing something from another country, too," said Chloe.

"This should be good," I whispered to Robbie.

"I'm sure it's something good old nana brought her from one of her trips."

"I'm bringing one hundred small, glass animals," said Chloe. "They're really special. My nana got them for me when she went to Italy."

Robbie turned and smiled at me. "What'd I tell you?"

"Aren't they breakable?" I asked.

"Oh, yes. They are very delicate. I have to wrap each one very carefully in bubble wrap."

"That seems like a lot of work."

"It is! I spent over an hour last night wrapping them, and I'm only about halfway through."

Robbie made the cuckoo sign again with his finger and giggled.

"I'll finish today when I get home from school. I can't wait for you to see them. I know you're just going to love them!" Chloe said, clapping her hands.

"Do we have a choice?" I whispered to Robbie.

We both laughed.

That girl just talks and talks and talks. I think she really likes the sound of her voice.

"How about you, Robbie?" asked Jessie. "What are you going to bring?"

"I think I'm going to bring my gem and mineral collection."

Robbie is a science genius. He knows everything about everything. He has all kinds of interesting collections. He probably had a hard time choosing what to bring.

"Where do you get the rocks?"

"I get them from different places. Sometimes I get them when I go on trips, some of them are from that store, Timeless Treasures, at the mall, but most of them my mom gets for me. She works for the Natural History Museum."

"You're so lucky," Jessie said. "I bet you have some really cool ones."

"Yeah. My favorite is a piece of prehistoric lava rock from a volcano."

"Wow! That must be really old!"

"It is! I have the whole collection labeled, so you'll know what each thing is when you see it."

"How about you, Freddy? What are you going to bring?"

"I have no idea. You all have really cool things to bring, and I have nothing."

I turned and stared out the window. This hundredth-day celebration was turning into a disaster! I only had one day left and not one good idea!

CHAPTER 5

Suzie to the Rescue?

When I got home from school, I went straight to my room. I didn't feel like talking to anybody. I lay down on my bed and looked up at the ceiling. I needed some quiet time to think.

"Hey, Shark Breath!" Suzie yelled as she pounded on my door. "I need the ruler for my math homework."

So much for quiet time. "Go away! I don't have it!"

"Yes, you do!"

"No, I don't!"

I heard the door handle start to turn, so I leaped off my bed to hold the door closed, but it was too late. Suzie had already pushed her way in.

"This is my room!" I shouted. "Get out!"

"Not until you give me the ruler."

"I told you I don't have your stupid ruler!" I shoved her toward the door. "Now get out of my room!"

"I know you have it, and I'm not leaving until you give it to me," Suzie said, folding her arms across her chest.

"Fine," I said. "Then you can stand there all day because I don't have it." Then I turned away and went back to sit on my bed.

Suzie stood perfectly still and stared at me for a minute without saying anything.

I looked up at her. "What?"

"That's it?"

"What do you mean?"

"I mean you're not going to fight with me anymore about the ruler?"

I sighed a great big sigh. "Nope."

"What's gotten into you? You never give up that easily."

"I don't have time today. I have a lot more important things to worry about."

"You?" Suzie said, chuckling. "What could you have to worry about that's so important?"

"The hundredth day of school!"

"Oh, right. That's tomorrow."

"And I still have nothing to bring!" I buried my face in my pillow.

Suzie tapped my shoulder. "Freddy?"

"Just leave me alone," I said into the pillow.

"Freddy?" she said again.

"I said to leave me alone!"

"I have an idea."

"You do?" I said, turning slowly to look at her. She had a big grin on her face.

"It's a great idea, and I'll even help you with it."

I sat up. "You would?"

"Of course. Don't I always?"

I stared at her.

"What's it worth to you?" she said

"Just tell me what you want, Suzie. I don't have all day."

"I get to choose the video games for a week."

"A week?"

Suzie nodded.

"How about two days?"

"Then you can come up with your own idea. It's a week or nothing," she said, holding up her pinkie for a pinkie swear.

At this point I didn't have much choice. Time

was running out. "Deal," I said as we locked pinkies. I had just doomed myself to a week of pink ponies and fashion makeovers.

"So?"

"So what?"

"So what's this great idea of yours?"

"Cookies," Suzie said smiling.

"Cookies? You already came up with that idea last night."

"No, I didn't."

"Yes, you did. You suggested animal crackers, remember? And I said that I thought they would break before I got them to school." I flopped back down on my bed. "Thanks for getting my hopes up for nothing."

Suzie sat down on the bed next to me. "Freddy, will you just listen to me for a minute? I'm not talking about cookies you buy at the store."

"Then what are you talking about? Could you speak English, please?" I was starting to get really frustrated.

"I'm talking about *homemade* cookies," Suzie said, grinning.

"Homemade cookies?"

"Yeah. Homemade chocolate-chip cookies."

I licked my lips. "Yummy." Maybe she was on to something here.

"You can bring in one hundred homemade chocolate-chip cookies."

"That's an awesome idea, Suzie!"

"I know," she said, smiling.

"The kids are going to love it!" I said, jumping around my room. "How did you come up with that idea?"

"I don't know. It just popped into my head."

"Well, I'm sure glad it did, because that is going to be the best hundredth-day idea ever!" I did a little dance.

"What are you doing, weirdo?"

"My happy dance."

"Save the dancing for later. Right now we have to convince Mom that this is a good idea."

"Oh, I forgot about that," I said, hanging my head. "She'll never let us do it."

"Why not?"

"Because it's too much work, and there isn't enough time."

"We have all afternoon, and I said I would help you."

"You will? You're the best sister in the whole world!" I said, throwing my arms around her and giving her a great big hug.

"I know," Suzie said. "Now let's get to work!"

CHAPTER 6

Cookie Craziness

Suzie and I ran downstairs to the kitchen. My mom was there, talking on the telephone.

"Mom! Mom!" I yelled, jumping up and down and waving my arms. "Suzie has the best idea!"

"Just one minute, Freddy, I'm on the phone."

I tried to wait, but my mom wouldn't get off the phone. "Mom," I said, tapping her shoulder. "It's really important."

"I'll be done in a second, Freddy. You need to be patient."

"Don't bug her while she's on the phone,"

Suzie whispered in my ear, "or she'll never agree to do the cookies."

I knew Suzie was right, but it was so hard to wait.

Finally my mom hung up. "So what's this great idea of Suzie's?"

"Suzie thought of something awesome I could bring for the hundredth-day celebration."

"Oh really? That's wonderful! What is it?"

"One hundred cookies."

"You're right. That is a great idea. You can even share them with your friends."

This was going a lot smoother than I thought it would. "So I can bring one hundred cookies?"

"Of course you can. Let me just get my purse, and I'll take you to the store to buy them."

Ugh, I knew this was too good to be true. "Uh, Mom . . ."

"Yes?"

"I was planning on bringing one hundred homemade cookies."

"Homemade cookies? But, Freddy, honey, we don't have a lot of time. The hundredth day is tomorrow. Let's just go buy some."

"But that's not the same," I whined.

"How about if we get them at the bakery instead of the market? They can put them in one of those pink bakery boxes. That will make them look special."

"I really wanted to make homemade chocolate-chip cookies."

"It's already four o'clock in the afternoon."

"I know, but Suzie said that she would help me."

"I don't know. That's a lot of cookies."

"We can do it, Mom," Suzie piped in. "How many cookies are in one batch?"

"I think about twenty-five."

"So that's only . . . four batches."

"Wow! Good for you for doing that math so quickly in your head, Suzie," my mom said.

"Thanks. I know that there are four quarters in a dollar, so four twenty-fives make one hundred."

"I'm impressed."

Suzie smiled.

"Well, I guess if we all work together, we

can do it," my mom said, "but we have to get started right away. You two go wash your hands. I'm going to get all the ingredients out." We ran to wash our hands and zoomed back. My mom gathered all the ingredients and set them on the kitchen table.

"Is everyone ready?" my mom asked.

"Ready!" we said.

We spent most of the afternoon making the cookies. We measured, stirred, and baked. It was a lot of work, but we had fun.

As we put the last batch in the oven, we did one final count to make sure we had exactly one hundred. "Ninety-eight, ninety-nine, one-hundred!"

"One hundred, one hundred, one hundred!" I sang, and then I started to dance.

"Freddy, what is that?" my mom asked, laughing.

"Don't you know? That's his happy dance," answered Suzie.

"I'm glad you're so happy, Freddy."

"This was the best idea ever! Thank you, Mom. Thank you, Suzie," I said, giving each of them a hug. "You're the best!"

"You're welcome, sweetie," said my mom.

Suzie looked at me and started laughing.

"What's so funny?"

"You look like a ghost!"

"Huh?"

"You're covered in flour!"

"So are you!" I said, laughing.

"Well, let's get this kitchen cleaned up, and then the two of you can go take your baths."

As we were cleaning up, my dad came home from work. "Something smells good in here," he said as he came into the kitchen.

"We're making chocolate-chip cookies."

"Oh, my favorite. It's my lucky day."

And before any of us could say a word, he picked one up off a finished tray and popped it in his mouth!

CHAPTER 7

Disaster!

"No! No! No!" I screamed, lunging toward my dad.

My dad froze.

"Give me the cookie! Give me the cookie!" I yelled, shaking my dad's arm.

"Freddy, what is the matter with you?"

"I need that cookie. Give it back, now!"

"I don't think I can do that."

"Why not?'

"Because it's in my stomach. I ate it."

"Oh, no, no, no!" I sobbed. "Now everything's ruined!"

"Would someone mind telling me what is going on here?" my dad asked.

"You just ate part of Freddy's hundredth day project," said Suzie.

"What?"

"Freddy was making one hundred cookies to bring into school, and you just ate one of them."

"Wah! Wah! Wah!" I wailed.

"Oh, Freddy, I had no idea. I'm so sorry."

I couldn't stop crying. "WAAAAAHHHHHH! Now I can't take them."

"Why can't you take the rest of them?"

"Because now I don't have one hundred. Mrs. Wushy said we had to bring in one hundred of something. No more, no less."

"How about making one more?"

"Unfortunately, we don't have any batter left," said my mom. "We just used up the last little bit."

"WAAAAHHHHHH!!!"

"Come here, Freddy," my dad said, picking

67

me up off the floor. "There must be something we can do."

"There's nothing. Nothing you can do. And now I have nothing to bring to school for the hundredth-day celebration tomorrow."

I yanked myself away from my dad and ran upstairs to my room. I slammed the door, plopped down on my bed, buried my face in my pillow, and cried . . . and cried . . . and cried.

I thought I heard a knock on my door, but I ignored it.

I heard the knock again.

"Go away!" I yelled.

"Freddy, can we come in?"

"I said go away! I don't want to talk to anybody right now."

The door handle slowly started to turn.

"Did you not hear me? I said go away!"

"We just wanted to talk to you for a minute," said my mom.

"Is Dad with you?"

"Yes."

"Well, I don't want to talk to him."

"Freddy, honey, that was a mistake. You know Daddy didn't eat the cookie on purpose."

"But that mistake ruined everything!"

My dad came into the room. "Freddy, just give me a minute."

He sat down on my bed. I turned the other way and buried my face in my pillow. "Freddy,

I am so sorry about what happened. I had no idea those cookies were part of your project."

I didn't say anything.

"You know I would never have touched them if I knew that."

I still didn't respond.

"Sometimes things in life don't go the way we planned, and we have to make another plan."

I rolled over and looked at him with tears in my eyes. "I don't have another plan, and the celebration is tomorrow!"

"Don't worry. We'll think of something."

"I can't think of anything!"

"Maybe Suzie can help us."

"She already did. The cookies were her idea."

"Well then, maybe she has some more good ideas."

"I doubt it," I mumbled.

"I just might surprise you," Suzie said as she walked into my room, hiding something behind her.

I sat up in bed. "Really?"

"Really," she said, smiling.

"What do you have behind your back?"

"Plan B."

"Plan B?"

"Yep."

"Well, what is it?" I said anxiously.

She pulled a jar out from behind her back.

"What's in that jar?"

"Buttons!"

"Buttons?"

"Yes. This is Grammy Rose's button jar. She used to collect buttons because she did a lot of sewing. It's where Mom found the button for your pants this morning."

"Cool," I said. "How many buttons do you think are in there?"

"At least a thousand, probably," said my mom. She opened the jar and carefully spilled some of the buttons out on the night table.

"Wow! Look at all those colors and sizes," I said. "She must have been collecting them for a long time."

"She did. She collected them for years."

"Why did she give them all to you, Mom?" Suzie asked.

"Well, it's harder for her to see now, so she doesn't do much sewing anymore. She thought we might like to use them for art projects and things like that."

"Why didn't you tell us about them before?"

"I forgot we had them," my mom said, "until I found them this morning."

"You could bring one hundred buttons to school," Suzie said.

"What's so great about buttons?" I asked. "Buttons are boring."

"But these aren't just any buttons," said my mom. "These are special buttons."

"What's so special about them?"

"Some of them are really old."

"Really?'

"In fact," said my dad, "there's a button in that jar that's from Grandpa Dave's army uniform from World War Two."

"Wow! That's cool."

"There's also a button in there from your great-grandmother's wedding dress," my mom said. "It's over one hundred years old."

I jumped off the bed and ran to give Suzie a hug. "Thanks, Suzie. What would I do without you?" Then I whispered in her ear, "What do I owe you for this one?'

"Nothing. This one's on me."

I smiled and turned back to my parents.

"Are there any other special buttons in that jar?" I asked.

"The jar is full of them. I can tell you lots of stories about these buttons."

"What are we waiting for?" I said. "Let's start counting!"

CHAPTER 8

The Hundredth Day

My mom, my dad, and Suzie had helped me count out one hundred of the coolest buttons. My mom even dumped out the rest of the buttons so I could bring mine to school in my grandma's blue-glass jar. We also packed up the ninety-seven cookies that were left (Suzie and I had each eaten one), so I could share them with the class.

When I got to school, there was a sign on

the classroom door that said "Happy 100th Day! You've all come a long way!" Throughout the day we did lots of special hundredth day activities. We made necklaces with one hundred pieces of cereal. We made a headband with one hundred tallies on it. We made a paper chain with one hundred links. We did puzzles with one hundred pieces. We wrote our names one hundred times. Finally it was time to share the hundred things we had brought in. We all went and sat in a big circle on the rug.

"Okay, everyone, let's settle down," said Mrs. Wushy. "I know you are all very excited and can't wait to share what you've brought. Who would like to go first?"

"Me, oh, me!! Me, me, me!!!" Chloe shouted, shaking her hand wildly in the air.

"Chloe, you need to remember that when your hand goes up, your mouth stays closed. I'm going to choose someone who has a quiet hand. Robbie, would you like to go first?"

"Sure," said Robbie. "I brought one hundred rocks and minerals from my collection," he said, pulling a large plastic container out of his bag.

Everyone ooohed and aaahhed.

"I have more at home, but I brought my

favorites, and I labeled each one so that every-body would know what they are."

"Why don't you tell us about a couple of them," said Mrs. Wushy.

"Well, OK, let's see," said Robbie, picking up a black rock. "This is a piece of volcanic rock that is formed when lava cools. I got it when I went hiking on a real volcano—Mt. Saint Helens, in Washington State."

"Hiking on a volcano," Max snickered. "You can't hike on a volcano."

"Of course you can't hike on it when it's erupting, because you would get killed, but if it's dormant—that means sleeping—you can walk on it."

Robbie is such a genius. I can't believe my best friend is so smart!

"That is fascinating," said Mrs. Wushy. "How about telling us about one more?"

Robbie picked up a gold nugget.

"Oh my gosh! Is that real gold! Where did you get it?" Chloe squealed.

"It looks like real gold, but it isn't. It's something called fool's gold. It's actually a mineral called pyrite."

"It sure fooled you," Max laughed, wagging his finger at Chloe.

"It did not!"

"Oh yes it did."

"OK," said Mrs. Wushy. "Enough, you two."

"Who would like to go next?"

"Me, oh me!! Me, me, me!!!" Chloe shouted again.

"Doesn't she ever learn?" I whispered to Robbie.

"Chloe, I will not call on any 'me-me's,'" said Mrs. Wushy. "Unless you can raise your hand quietly, you will not get a turn. Jessie, would you like to go next?"

"Hey!" Max blurted out. "Why does she get to go next?"

"Because she's sitting quietly."

Jessie pulled a small woven sack from behind her back. "My *abuela*, you know, my grandma, let me bring her special collection of worry dolls."

"What are worry dolls?"

"They're these tiny little dolls that you keep

in a pouch and tell all of your worries to. That way *you* don't have any worries. The dolls hold them all for you."

"Really? Where did she get them?"

"They come from Central America. She's been collecting them since she was a little girl."

I raised my hand.

"Yes, Freddy?"

"I brought something from my grandma, too."

"Really? Well then, why don't you go next?" Chloe groaned.

I pulled the button jar and the bag of cookies out from under my shirt where I had been hiding them.

"Hey, Mrs. Wushy," Chloe whined. "Freddy has two things. That's not fair."

"Why don't we let Freddy tell us about what he has."

I held up the button jar. "This is my Grammy Rose's button jar."

"Buttons?" Max snorted. "What's so great about dumb, old buttons?"

"Max, that is not polite," said Mrs. Wushy.

"These are not just any buttons, Max," I said. "These are special buttons."

"Oh yeah? What's so special about them?"

I held up the button that was from my grandpa's uniform. "See this button? My grandpa fought in World War Two, and this button is from his army uniform."

"Really?" said Max.

"Yep. Really," I said, smiling.

"That's cool."

I held up a small white button. "This button

is from my great-grandmother's wedding dress. She got married in Russia over one hundred years ago."

"Your buttons are real pieces of history," said Mrs. Wushy. "You are lucky your grandma saved them and passed them down to your family. Maybe later today you can share some more of your button stories."

I smiled.

"You still didn't tell us what's in that other bag," said Chloe.

"You mean this one?" I said, patting the cookie bag.

"Yeah, what's in there?"

"A mistake."

"A mistake? What are you talking about, Freddy?"

"Well, you see, I made one hundred choco-late-chip cookies to bring in today, but then my dad ate one by mistake, so I only had ninety-nine. Mrs. Wushy said we had to bring in one hundred things, no more, no less, so I had to think of something else to bring. I worked really hard making the cookies, so I brought them in to share with everybody, if that's OK with Mrs. Wushy."

"Oh, Freddy, I'm so sorry you went to all that trouble," said Mrs. Wushy. "Of course you can share them with the class. What an unexpected treat!"

I passed out the cookies, and everyone gobbled them up.

"These are really yummy," said Chloe.

"This is the best mistake I've ever eaten!" Jessie said, giggling.

"You can say that again," said Max, stuffing more cookie into his mouth.

I laughed and shook my head.

After all that worrying, the One Hundredth Day of School turned out to be one hundred percent perfect!

DEAR READER,

I have been a teacher for many years, and every
year I celebrate the 100th day of school with my
students. We make a special snack with 100 treats
in it. We make a headband with 100 tallies on it, and
we make a necklace with 100 pieces of cereal. And
just like Freddy, each child in my class must bring
in 100 of something. My students love sharing their
special 100th-day collections. One year a little boy
brought in 100 postcards from all over the world.
Another time, a little girl brought in 100 beautiful
pieces of sea glass. Each year I look forward to seeing
what my students bring in.

I hope you have as much fun reading *The One
Hundredth Day of School!* as I had writing it.

HAPPY READING!

Abby Klein

Freddy's Fun Pages

FREDDY'S SHARK JOURNAL

There are about 400 different species of sharks, but they all have certain features in common.

Sharks have gills for breathing underwater.

Sharks have one or two dorsal fins on their backs.

A shark's skin is covered in tiny, thorn-like hooks called *denticles*.

Sharks have a pair of pectoral and pelvic fins.

Most sharks have long, pointed snouts.

ONE HUNDRED LINKS

Make a chain with one hundred links
to decorate your bedroom.

SUPPLIES: colored construction paper
tape or glue

DIRECTIONS:

1. Cut 100 one-inch-wide strips of
colored construction paper about
four to five inches long.

2. For the first loop, glue or tape
the two ends of one strip together.

3. Then take another strip,
put it through the loop you
just made, and then glue
or tape the ends closed.

4. Repeat step 3 until you
have used up all your strips.

5. Hang in your bedroom.

FREDDY'S 100TH DAY SNACK

To make Freddy's special trail mix you will need:

 10 Round cereal bits

10 Chocolate chips

10 Small colored candies

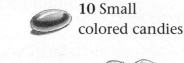

10 Small cereal squares

10 Mini pretzels

10 Fish-shaped crackers

 10 Mini marshmallows

10 Small square cheese crackers

10 Raisins

10 Sunflower seeds

Put it all in a baggie and shake 100 times.
(Like Freddy, you can choose any ten each of
whatever small snack foods you like best.)
Eat and enjoy!

100 TIMES!

Test yourself! Can you do each
of these things 100 times?

1. Clap your hands

2. Jump up and down

3. Snap your fingers

4. Blink your eyes

5. Do a jumping jack

6. Say your name

7. Tap your head

8. Hop on one foot

9. Stomp your feet

10. Kiss your mom or dad!

Have you read all about Freddy?

Don't miss any of Freddy's funny adventures!